THE ROYAL ESTATE

AANYA SHARMA

Made with ♥ on the Notion Press Platform
www.notionpress.com

“"Drama doesn’t just walk into your life. You either create it, invite it or you associate with people who love to bring it into your life."”

Contents

Prologue

Once upon a time in the spectacular Akkadian Kingdom, there lived a beautiful young princess named Cassandra Donnelly. She was the daughter of King Robert and Queen Alexandra Donnelly. The King and Queen were blessed with four children, 3 son and a daughter. The eldest son's name was Augustus Donnelly, and he was 28 years old, the second son's name was Fedrick Donnelly, and he was 25 years old, the youngest son's name was Cyrus Donnelly, and he was 23 years old and then the youngest of all was Cassandra Donnelly, she was 20 years old. Cassandra was the only princess of the Akkadian kingdom. Her brothers adored her. They were always there to protect her and make her happy. She had always been the kindest one among the royals. She was not allowed to participate in sword fighting but her stubbornness made her parents allow it. Her father and mother both were strict but loved her dearly. She never really enjoyed royalty. In her mind, it would have been better if she had been born in an ordinary village house rather than in a castle. Unlike other princesses this young princess hated royalty. And when it came to restrictions she was averse to them. She was excellent at sword fighting. The chief commander of the kingdom, Nikolai Jefferson, taught her sword fighting. He was 24 years old. Nikolai was a cold, reserved, and loyal person. The young princess always had eyes for the chief commander but never made a move since she knew there was no way her father would let her be with someone who is not a part of the royal family. But the thing she didn't know was that it was not just her, but the chief commander also felt the same but never admitted it since

he knew she would never be his. The princess often used to sneak out of the castle and go to her favorite place just to escape from all the royalty for some time. The Akkadian kingdom was beautiful and peaceful. But like any other kingdom, this kingdom also had many enemies. But the biggest enemy of the Akkadian kingdom was the Mordor Kingdom ruled by king Joseph Maxwell, who was 25 years old. Joseph was young but was one of the most feared kings. He wanted to be the most powerful, most feared and the most prime person in the world. He was known for his dark and scary aura.

1

The Princess

It was a beautiful morning when the princess woke up with sunlight hitting her face. She groans.

Cassandra: (sits up)(yawns) good morning world.

Just when she wakes up the maids enter.

Maid: Good morning your Majesty. (bows)

Cassandra: Good morning Nadia.

(Nadia is Cassandra's maid. She is the closest to her.)

Nadia: Your majesty shall we prepare for your bath?

Cassandra: Yes, yes I don't plan on slumbering more. You may prepare the bath.

The maids start to prepare for the bath, while Cassandra gets up. After the bath, the maids dress up Cassandra in a beautiful wine-colored dress. After getting ready Cassandra heads toward the dining hall. She sees her parents and brothers already present there.

Cassandra: Good morning my majesties. (greets everyone)

Everyone except Cassandra: Good morning dear.

Just then the commander arrives.

Nikoli: Good morning your majesties. (bows)(looks at Cassandra)Good morning princess.

Cassandra: Good morning commander. (Bows slightly)

King Robert: Nikolai, how's the situation at the borders? Have the Maxwells ceased the attacks?

Federick: The attacks?!!

Augustus: Yes, Fedrick attacks. The Mordor kingdom is doing it again, they have been attacking the outskirts villages.

Cyrus: Why do they always attack the outskirts and then stop?

Cassandra: They are testing our patience brother, they want us to be the ones to attack them first and enter their territory cause they are the most powerful in their territory. They are just playing games, nothing else.

Nikolai: I agree with the princess.

Just then the maids arrive with the food.

Queen Alexandra: Okay everyone enough with the Maxwells now let's have our breakfast.

Nikolai: I'll take my leave now your majesty.

Nikolai exits the hall. And everybody else has their breakfast.

After breakfast, Cassandra decides to go to the library.

At the library

Cassandra is reading books and Nadia is preparing tea for her.

Nadia: Your majesty, may I ask you something?

Cassandra: Yes of course Nadia, what is it?

Nadia: Your majesty why do you always sneak out of the castle at night? You can just tell everyone that you are going out, and, of course, you can also take security with you. Then why do you do it?

Cassandra: Nadia, the only reason I do it is to escape this royalty for some time, just to live as "Cassandra" and not as the princess of the Akkadian kingdom. Even though it is just for a little time, it is enough for me to have a peaceful sleep at night. And you are right I can just tell everyone and take security with me but that won't allow me to escape my royalty because the security would be there to protect the princess. And do you think that father would allow me to go out every night, that too such a quiet place? And honestly yes he would allow me to go for a few days but after a few days. (chuckles)

Nadia: Ohh my dear princess, you have as many miseries as you have good fortunes. Yet as far as I can think, people who have too much are just as sick as those who are ill and starving by having nothing with them. It is not a bad fortune, then, to be placed between the two extremes of having too much and too little. The man who has too much well soon becomes grey- haired but he who has just enough wealth lives longer.

Cassandra: Well spoken Nadia. I guess you have been reading too.

Nadia:(chuckles) You caught me, princess.

Both laugh and head back to the castle. And have their lunch.

After Lunch, the princess went to the garden for her sword fighting practice.

At the garden

Cassandra entered the garden and saw Nikolai standing there with his back facing her.

Cassandra: Good afternoon Commander.

Nikolai: Afternoon princess. Shall we start!?

Cassandra: yeah Sure Commander.

Nikolai and Cassandra started fighting. Every time Cassandra attacked Nikolai he dodged her attack effortlessly. Cassandra grew frustrated and attacked the commander with her full strength. But while attacking

him she slipped and fell on top of the commander. The commander and Cassandra made eye contact and just when the commander was about to speak, Queen Alexandra called out for Cassandra. The princess hurriedly stood up and answered her mother.

Nikolai: Umm princess you should go. That's enough for today.

Cassandra: yes I'll get going.

Cassandra leaves.

Nikolai: Why do you always do this to my heart princess. (in his mind)

Cassandra: Why do you always do this to my heart commander. (in her mind).

After this Nikolai left for the throne room.

In the throne room

King Robert: Nikolai, what's the information about the attack?

Nikolai: Your majesty the attacks have ceased. The Mordor commander Peter Lofferson left a note for us saying that they are terminating the attacks for now but soon they will give us a massive surprise.

Augustus: What surprise!!??

Nikolai: they are preparing to attack your majesty. But I am sure that would take some time as they just finished a war with their rival kingdom.

King Robert: That's a good opportunity for us to strengthen our relations with the neighboring kingdoms so that they can be helpful during the war.

Everyone starts to figure out ways to resolve all their rivalries and make friends with the kingdoms as much as possible.

Federick: Father, what about the Latervia kingdom? They are strongest after us and the maxwells.

King Robert: I know son and for that, I do have something which may help.

Cyrus: What father??

KingRobert: Marriage.

Federick/Cyrus: marriage!!!??? who's!!???

King Robert: Agustus's.

Augustus: Father–

King Robert: Son I know this may seem cruel but this is the only way to be on good terms with them. Their daughter Natalia is very beautiful. So son are you willing to sacrifice your dream of first finding love and then getting married for the goodness of your kingdom?

Augustus: (sighs) I am ready father. My top priority is to protect the kingdom. And if this is helpful for the kingdom in any way, I am ready for it.

King Robert: That's my son. Nikolai send a letter to the Latveria kingdom proposing the marriage of my son Augustus Donnelly and their daughter Jessica Cyler.

Nikolai: Alright your majesty.

Leaves the throne room.

At night when Cassandra got to know about the marriage, she was irate and wanted to talk to her father but Augustus stopped her.

Cassandra: But why brother?! Marriage is not a joke. How can he just set your marriage like this? Just to bring peace between the kingdoms.

Augustus: it's for the kingdom sister—

Cassandra: but you have your personal life too brother. You marry who you want to marry not just for the kingdom but for love, for yourself.

Augustus: Cass this is the first time father asked me for something and I am not gonna let him down.

Cassandra: but—

Augustus: I am gonna marry the princess of Latveria kingdom and that's final. I don't want any conversation on this again. Understood.

Cassandra: yes brother.

Cassandra goes to her chamber.

> ***"Sacrifice is a part of life. It's supposed to be. It's not something to regret. It's something to aspire to""***

In her room

Cassandra: Aaarrrgggghhh this is why I despise loyalty. You have nothing above your kingdom, nothing. (sighs) I need a break.

Cassandra takes a black robe, sneaks out of the castle, and goes to her secret place.

At Cassandra's secret place

Cassandra reaches the place. When she reached she found a tall figure standing there with his back facing her. Cassandra was surprised as no one used to come here other than her. So she asked him:

Cassandra: who are you?

The figure turned around. And when she saw who it was she became surprised and a bit scared as her secret of sneaking out was now revealed to the person.

The person: So this is where you sneak out to every day huh!.

WHO IS THE PERSON? WILL HE TELL THE KING ABOUT PRINCESS SNEAKING OUT.? IS HE GONNA HARM THE PRINCESS? WHAT'S GONNA HAPPEN? WILL THE PRINCESS BE OKAY?.................

2

The Protector

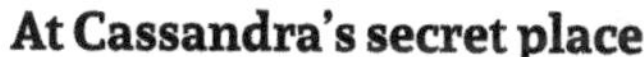

At Cassandra's secret place

……-so this is where you sneak out every day huh.

Cassandra: Co-Commander!!!

Nikolai: princess

Cassandra: Wh-What are you doing here?

Nikolai: Well princess, what did think that someone would go out of the castle every night and I wouldn't even know about it?

Cassandra: You knew????!!!

Nikolai: Yes I knew that someone used to sneak out of the castle every night just didn't know who it was. Well, guess what I know now.

Cassandra: Commander please don't tell father about this, please commander. I'll do whatever you want. But please, don't tell father he'll be very mad.

Nikolai: Okay princess as you say but you have to promise me that you won't sneak out at night again.

Cassandra: I can't do that.

Nikolai: Well then I guess I'll have to tell your majesty about this little habit of yours.

Cassandra: Are you threatening me right now commander??

Nikolai: (chuckles) Princess all I want is your protection—

Cassandra: (shouts)BUT I DON'T NEED YOUR PROTECTION, I DON'T NEED ANYONE'S PROTECTION.

Nikolai:(sighs) Princess please try to understand. You are too precious to be harmed.

Cassandra looks at Nikolai. They make 2-second eye contact. Then Cassandra walks back to the castle.

Cassandra: I'll try to stop sneaking out but I can't promise you anything. (while walking away)

Nikolai: (smiles)sure princess.

Nikolai also leaves.

In Cassandra's room

Cassandra: Why does he have to be like this? (fake cries) I can't even go to my favorite place. Nadia why does he do this, it's not like he is my husband or something.

Nadia:(chuckles) Princess you know I sometimes wonder if you've grown up or not. You're still a small kid inside the body of an adult.

Cassandra:(pouts)

Nadia:(smiles) Princess you should sleep. Good night. (leaves the room)

Cassandra:(sighs) Night.

The next day

In the throne room

Nikolai enters with a letter in his hands.

Nikolai: Good Morning your majesty.

King Robert: Morning Commander. What news have you brought, Commander?

Nikolai: We received a letter from the Latervia kingdom, your majesty.

King Robert: Ohh really, read it out, commander.

"*Nikolai: "Dear king Robert*

We received your letter. And we are very delighted to say that we accept your proposal for the marriage of our daughter and your son. We look forward to discussing the arrangement of the marriage by inviting you over for dinner at our palace on the following night.

King Henry Cyler of the Latervia kingdom."

***Cyrus: That's a piece of great news!!*"**

King Robert: It is indeed.

After this, the news about the marriage of the eldest son of the king spread in the whole kingdom.

The next day

While going to the Latervia kingdom in the cart.

As the whole royal family was going to the latervia kingdom. The king and queen were sitting in one cart, Cassandra and Augustus in the second cart, and Fedrick and Cyrus in the third cart.

Inside the second cart

Cassandra: Brother.

Augustus: Yes princess.

Cassandra: Look, brother, I am only going to allow your marriage if you promise that we'll be the same, you'll spend time with me too, and not just your wife and your wifey won't come between us. And also you won't forget your poor little sister.

Augustus:(chuckles)Don't worry princess, my marriage won't change a thing between us, and "my wifey" won't come between us. And also I won't forget my poor little sister. Okay!?

Cassandra: Okie. (cutely)

Augustus chuckles and ruffles her hair.

After this, they enter the castle and have dinner with the Cylers, Augustus's and Jessica's marriage gets fixed. Augustus and Jessica fell in love with each other at first sight.

> ***""Happy marriages begin when we marry the ones we love and they blossom when love the ones we marry""***

3

The Confession

On the wedding day

The past days have been extremely hectic for the whole royal family as the preparations for the marriage were going on. But it all went well. Currently, Augustus and Jessica are standing on the stage, taking their vows and Cassandra is standing beside Nikolai.

Cassandra: I hope one day I also have a beautiful and happy marriage like this with the person I love.

Nikolai:(stares at Cassandra)You can marry whoever you want princess.

Cassandra;(chuckles) I don't think so, the person you want to marry always doesn't want to marry you.

The wedding ends.

2 days later

Augustus and Natalia have been enjoying their married life for the past two days whereas Cassandra has grown more competitive to defeat the commander in sword fighting.

In the garden, while practicing with the commander

Cassandra: Commander may I ask you something?

Nikolai: Sure princess what is it?

Cassandra: Do you have someone in your life?

Nikolai: What do you mean princess!?

Cassandra: Like a lover or someone you love.

Nikolai: (chuckles)Well princess, I have devoted my life to the kingdom, the kingdom is my top priority and I don't think a person should be falling in love unless he can make it his top priority.

Cassandra: (nods) I fully agree.

Cassandra: (in her mind) God! How do I even make him fall in love with me when he simply loves THE KINGDOM more than anything!!!.

3 days later

These three days have been very challenging for Cassandra. Her feelings for Nikolai have been growing too much and in these three days, she decided to tell Nikolai about her feelings for him. She had enough.

To tell Nikolai her feelings she took him to her secret place saying she wanted to tell him something important.

At the secret place

Nikolai: What is it, princess?? What do you wanna tell me??

Cassandra: (takes a deep breath) I Love You, Commander. (closes her eyes)

She waits for a second for Nikolai to say something but all she hears is silence so she opens her eyes and looks at Nikolai who is in utter shock.

Nikolai: Princess, what are you saying!!??

Cassandra: I love you, Nikolai.

Nikolai: No! No! Princess, you can't love me.

Cassandra: But I do!!

Nikolai: No you can't princess we can never be together.

Cassandra: We can be Nikolai—

Nikolai: No we can't

Cassandra: BUT WHY!!!!

Nikolai: BECAUSE WE CAN'T!! I AM NOT EVEN FROM A ROYAL FAMILY AND THE KING, THE QUEEN, AND THE PEOPLE WOULD NEVER ACCEPT A RELATIONSHIP BETWEEN A PRINCESS AND A COMMANDER!!!!! try to understand princess.

Cassandra: Forget about the king, the people, forget about everyone. Tell me about yourself DO YOU LOVE ME!!??

Nikolai:..............

Cassandra: ANSWER ME, COMMANDER!!!

Nikolai: No, I don't. I don't love you princess.

Cassandra feels her heart shattered into pieces. After such a long time, she finally decided to tell the commander about her feelings but he doesn't even love her.

Cassandra: (broken voice)Yo-You don't??

Nikolai: No princess I don't and it would be better if you also don't. We can never be together.

Cassandra:(looks down)I didn't know what love felt like until I met you, but now I know what a broken heart feels like too.

Cassandra leaves the place.

(Nikolai knew he has feelings for Cassandra but he could never accept them as he knew it would only bring harm to him and the princess. He felt bad for hurting the princess.)

The next day

After what happened yesterday Cassandra was broken she felt like her world was torn apart. But she knew the reason why Nikolai rejected her. So she decided she won't back off that easily.

After lunch, as always Cassandra went to the garden for her sword fighting practice. And there she saw the commander but didn't show any emotion and started her practice with the commander.

Nikolai:(in his mind) I didn't expect her to come to the practice today. Well, then I guess she's tougher than I thought.

During the whole fight, Cassandra fought emotionlessly and powerfully. And not just that she defeated the commander for the first time....

Nikolai was lying on the ground with Cassandra's sword pointing at his neck. And then Cassandra finally spoke.

Cassandra: I know you love me, commander. But you just can't accept it knowing how dangerous it can be for us but believe me, commander, I'll do everything in my power to make you accept it, I promise you that.

Cassandra leaves the garden.

Nikolai: Why is she making it so hard for me!!?? (sighs)

> ***"It's hard to admit when you have fallen in love with someone who can't be yours."***

4 The Attack

It's been days since Cassandra has been trying to make Nikolai accept that he loves her but nothing seems to work. It's like if Cassandra is stubborn then Nikolai is even more stubborn. But Cassandra being Cassandra doesn't back off and keeps trying. Right now she is in the throne room talking with her father and once again trying to get some reaction from the commander.

In the throne room

Cassandra: Father.

King Robert: Yes princess.

Cassandra: Father I think I should get married. (looks at Nikolai for any reaction but he is still expressionless)

King Robert: What do you mean?

Cassandra: I mean I am old enough now to have a family of my own. What do you think?

King Robert: Well if you want to get married, I don't see any problem with that.

Cassandra looks at Nikolai to see if it affects him but he stands still and emotionless. Cassandra sighs, realizing her plan has flopped once again.

Cassandra: You know what father, just forget it I don't plan on getting married anymore. (gets up) I'll take my leave now. (bows and leaves)

As Cassandra leaves, Nikolai also leaves for his work. But when he goes out he suddenly gets pinned to the wall. It was Cassandra.

Cassandra: It really doesn't affect you right if I go marry someone else huh!.

Nikolai: Princess you can marry whoever you want. Who am I to say something?

Cassandra was now very mad. She had enough of him now.

Cassandra: I have had enough of you Nikolai. Is it that arduous to accept that you love me?

Nikolai was about to say something but Cassandra left before he could.

2 days later

It's been two days since that incident happened. And Cassandra hasn't talked to Nikolai since then. She hasn't even gone to her sword-fighting practice. Nikolai knew he had hurt her too much this time.

In the throne room

Nikolai: Your majesty, the attacks from the Mordor kingdom have increased too much and it doesn't look like they are planning to stop this time.

Queen Alexandra: Commander are you stating that there is a war coming?

Nikolai: There is a high possibility your majesty.

King Robert: Then we should prepare our forces.

Nikolai: Yes your majesty I have already started to work on that.

When Nikolai was about to say something else, a messenger entered the throne room.

King Robert: What is the message that you have brought???

Messenger: Your majesty the Mordor kingdom has declared war, they have entered the kingdom through secret tunnels and are marching towards the castle.

Cyrus/Fedrick: What!!???

Messenger: Yes your majesty.

Nikolai: Your majesty we should hurry.

King Robert: Yes yes commander.

The messenger was about to leave but Augustus stops him.

Augustus: Is the king there too??

Messenger: Yes your majesty, the king and the commander both are leading their armies.

Augustus: Shit!!

Everyone gets ready for the war. Cassandra said she wanted to be on the front but the king and princes didn't let her. Whereas Nikolai left for the place where the attacks were currently happening. Nikolai took 60% of the army with him because they were informed that they were losing. 40% of the army was left behind at the castle with the royal family.

At the place of the attack

Nikolai and the forces reach the place but they see that there were no soldiers, the Akkadian army was already defeated and there was no sign of the Mordor king or soldiers. Nikolai realized it was all a trap set by the Mordors. They knew if they attacked a place other than the castle before, most of the forces would be at that place and the castle would have less security.

Nikolai: Shit!!! Shit!!! This is all a TRAP!! EVERYONE MARCH BACK TO THE CASTLE!!..

Just when they were about to march back they got a message.

> "*The message:*
> *"The castle has been attacked, march back immediately."*"

WHAT WOULD HAPPEN NEXT???!! WILL THE COMMANDER BE ABLE TO REACH THE KINGDOM ON TIME!!!??? WILL THE AKKADIAN KINGDOM WIN THE WAR?? WILL THEY BE ABLE TO DEFEAT THE POWERFUL MORDOR KINGDOM??? WILL THEY ALL SURVIVE??!!

5

The Battle

At the castle

As the Mordors attacked the kingdom, everybody is currently fighting them.

King Robert was fighting with a soldier and defeated him very easily.

Augustus was attacked by two soldiers from the back and front, he kicked the one in the front and turned and quickly killed the back one. After killing him he killed the front one.

Cyrus and Fedrick were fighting together. Fedrick would strike the man and Cyrus would finish him off. They were fighting side by side.

Cassandra was defeating the soldiers very easily. She was striking the one near her and was shooting arrows at the one distant from her.

While Cassandra was fighting with a soldier suddenly another soldier came from behind and was about to strike her but before he could Nikolai came and knocked him down. Cassandra turned around. Cassandra and Nikolai looked at each other for a second, then started fighting side by side.

Too many soldiers were coming into the castle it was becoming difficult to fight inside.

Cyrus: Fedrick we need to block the main gate. They are too much.

Fedrick: Yes you are right let's go.

Fedrick and Cyrus went to the main gate and were about to block it but they saw a huge amount of army outside. So Fedrick got an idea.

Fedrick: Wait! Come with me!

Cyrus: Where??

Fedrick: Just come.

Fedrick and Cyrus gathered a lot of curtains and tied them together. They tied heavy rocks at the corners so that it doesn't flow up. Then they went to the terrace and threw the curtain down on the people. And then fired an arrow of fire on the curtain. They killed all the soldiers that were outside the castle. They did a high 5 when they succeeded.

The Akkadians were now winning. The strategy of Fedrick and Cyrus really helped. Just as they were about to win, the scream of the king was heard. Everybody looked at the king and saw a sword struck right through his stomach.

Cassandra/Augustus/Cyrus/Fedrick: FATHER!!!!!!!!

Just then a tall figure came out from behind the king. He had blue eyes, raven-colored hair, a masculine physique, and a scary and dark aura. Everybody figured out that it was the king of the Mordor Kingdom JOSEPH MAXWELL......

6

The Rival King

The Mordor king comes in front with his sword still on king Robert's neck.

Joseph: Evening everyone!!! (smiles evilly)

He pushes king Robert on his knees with the sword still on his neck. Augustus and Nikolai were about to go to him. But then he spoke.

Joseph: Nobody moves!! Or say goodbye to your dear king. (while pressuring the sword a bit)

Cassandra:(sternly) NOBODY MOVES.

Joseph smirks.

Joseph: So everyone let me introduce myself. Though I know you all already know me but still, it doesn't look good right?! (grins)

Joseph: I am Joseph Maxwell, the king of the Mordor Kingdom. And I am here to sign a treaty with you, The Akkadian Kingdom.

Cyrus: What treaty??

Joseph: Look kid The Mordor Kingdom and The Akkadian Kingdom are the most powerful kingdoms. Right?

Cyrus nods.

Joseph: So instead of fighting each other we should sign a treaty and rule side by side with no wars. Yeah. Look this way there will be peace and by not fighting with each other we can be more and more powerful. So here's a treaty that we don't attack each other and if one decides to break this treaty he shall face a dreadful death. (takes out some papers and throws them on the floor) The choice is all yours.

Augustus picks the treaty and looks at his father. King Robert nods.

Augustus: We'll sign this treaty. (signs it)

Joseph: Okay now ill take my leave your majesties. (he was about to remove his sword from the king's neck when he remembers something)

Joseph: Wait Wait I forgot one thing.

Fedrick: What?

Joseph: I'mma takes your princess with me.

Nikolai: WHAT!??

Joseph: Well first I was planning to marry the princess of the Latervia Kingdom. You know I need a partner too. But you guys already took her. So I'm gonna take your princess.

Nikolai: What nonsense!! Do you even know what you are saying?

Fedrick: Our sister is not a thing that you can take.

Augustus: King Joseph we would like you to leave now.

Joseph: (chuckles)Princess do you wanna come with me? (looks at Cassandra)

Cassandra: Why would I even come with a beast like you??

Joseph:(chuckles) You haven't even seen the real beast yet princess.

Joseph: MY DEAR AKKADIANS ARE YOU ALL FORGETTING THAT THE LIFE OF YOUR DEAR KING IS STILL IN MY HANDS HUH!

King Robert: You can just kill me but don't you dare touch my daughter.

Cassandra: Father—

King Robert: No Cassandra You. Won't. Go. With. Him.

Joseph: Well let me make it easy. Either the princess stays and the king dies or the princess goes with me and the king lives. The decision is all yours, princess. You are the one to decide. What you wanna choose?? Yourself or Your Father.

7 The Choice

Cassandra was in deep crisis. She had to choose between her and her father. It was a decision she never wanted to make and how could she, if she chooses herself her father will die which she will never let happen and if she chooses her father she'll have to go to the dangerous Mordor kingdom with the beast king, and god knows what he'll do to her. She knew she had to choose one, so she choose......

Cassandra: I'll go with you. But you have to promise you won't do anything bad to me.

Joseph: Of course princess, I am not that bad. I respect women.

King Robert: NO!! Cassandra, you will not go with him. I won't allow it. I would die happily if it is to save my daughter but I won't let her go into hell just to save myself.

Cassandra: I am sorry father but this time I can't listen to you. (Looks at joseph) I'll go with you.

Joseph: Let's go, princess. (removes the sword)

They were about to leave the castle.

King Robert: Cassandra!!

Cassandra:(looks back) I am sorry father but I did what was required. Goodbye.

Nikolai was about to come to Cassandra.

Joseph: Nope Commander You do not get to stop us.

They leave.

At the Mordor Kingdom

Cassandra and Joseph enter the palace. Joseph calls a maid and tells her to show Cassandra her room.

Joseph: Princess I would like you to take some rest for now. We'll talk later.

Cassandra doesn't say anything and silently walks away with the maid. After showing Cassandra the room the maid walks away and locks the door from the outside.

Inside The room

Cassandra: Aaarrghhh I don't know what's gonna happen next. This is so frustrating. (sighs) she even locked the door I can't even go outside. (groans)

After some time the maid comes inside the room with food.

Maid: Your majesty please have food.

Cassandra: (looks away) I don't want to.

Maid: Your majesty please the king wants you to eat.

Cassandra: I don't want to.

Maid: Please your majesty, the king has said.

Cassandra: I SAID I DON'T WANT TO EAT. I DON'T CARE IF YOUR KING HAS SAID OR WHOEVER HAS SAID, I DON'T WANNA EAT. LEAVE ME ALONE.

The maid sighs and leaves. When she went to the kitchen she saw joseph there.

Joseph: Did she eat?

Maid: No your majesty instead she shouted and asked to leave her alone.

Joseph: Did you tell her I said it?

Maid: She said she doesn't care. (looks down)

Joseph:(clenches his jaw) I guess the princess needs to be taught some manners.

Joseph goes to Cassandra's room.

In Cassandra's Room

Joseph: Cassandra Donnelly.

Cassandra: What??

Joseph: I didn't know you were this mannerless.

Cassandra: What??

Joseph: (walks closer to her) Don't you know you have to respect the king of the kingdom in which you stand? Do I need to teach you some manners princess?

Cassandra looks away.

Joseph: Princess, Did the cat get your tongue?

Cassandra: (faces him) Why should I respect You? You brought me here for no reason, You locked me in a room, and because of YOU, I am away from my family. Why. Should. I. Respect. You. Give me one reason.

Joseph: First of all princess I am not the reason you are here You yourself are the reason, YOU choose to come here okay?

Cassandra doesn't answer. She feels scared.

Joseph: Look princess I don't wanna be rude to you, but for that, you need to obey me okay? This is my kingdom, my castle, I am the one who makes the rules and you have to listen to me. Alright!?

Cassandra nods.

Joseph: If I am not doing anything to you doesn't mean I can't. Understood?

Cassandra: Y-Yes.

Joseph: Good. Now eat the food.

Cassandra eats the food. Joseph leaves. After eating the food Cassandra felt very tired so she decided to sleep.

The next day

Cassandra woke up to a maid shaking her.

Maid: Your Majesty the king is waiting for you for breakfast at the dining hall. Please get up, take a bath, and come downstairs.

Cassandra: I don't want to.

Joseph: (out of nowhere) Are you sure about that princess? (raises an eyebrow)

Cassandra turned towards him and saw him leaning against the door. She remembered what happened yesterday. And immediately said.

Cassandra: I am coming in 5 minutes.

Joseph:(chuckles) You better do.

At the dining hall

Joseph and Cassandra were having their breakfast when Joseph spoke.

Joseph: Listen princess I am not gonna make you a maid or tie you up or anything like that. Your gonna live the way used to live, as a princess only, okay? The only difference is gonna be that you'll be living in the Mordor kingdom rather than the Akkadian kingdom and you'll live with me instead of your family okay?

Cassandra nods.

Joseph: And if you try to escape or do anything stupid, I'll do all the things I said I won't. Understood?

Cassandra: Yes.

Joseph: hmm.

2 days later

Cassandra was in the Garden doing her sword fighting practice. She was bored she had nothing to do and no one to talk to, though she made friends with the maids, they were busy doing their chores and Joseph was also out of the castle. So she had nothing to do. While she was practicing suddenly Joseph came to her.

Joseph: What are you doing little princess?

Cassandra: Nothing just passing time. (points the sword at joseph) Do you wanna fight?

Joseph:(chuckles) Are you challenging me, princess?

Cassandra: Not exactly but yeah.

Joseph: Well I never say no to challenges.

They started fighting Cassandra attacked him a few times but he dodged them all.

Joseph: Woah!! You're good at this princess.

Cassandra: (smirks) I know.

Joseph chuckles and pushes Cassandra back by putting force on the sword.

Joseph: My turn.

Joseph starts attacking Cassandra. He attacked really fast and swiftly. Cassandra kept dodging his attacks. So he attacks very forcefully which leads to Cassandra Losing her balance and falling on the ground with Joseph on top of her. They looked at each other and Joseph chuckled and tucked her hair which were flying onto her face behind her ear and said.

Joseph: I won sweetheart.

He then got up and gave the princess a hand and made her stand up.

Joseph: Okay princess now I'll get going. Call me whenever you want to have a second round.

Cassandra felt weird. She felt deja vu. The same moment happened with Nikolai. She felt the same as she

felt with Nikolai. But how is this possible, she loves Nikolai but she hates Joseph. Then how could she feel the same? She couldn't understand why she was feeling that way. It was eating her up.

"*"There's a thin line between love and hate."*"

8

The Feelings

1 month later

In the Akkadian Kingdom

Everything's a mess in the Akkadian kingdom. The queen is crying remembering and missing her daughter, the princes are miserable without their sister, the king is taking all the blame on himself and the most miserable is Nikolai. He realized how much the princess's presence affected him, he realized how deep in love he was with the princess. There was no one to make him laugh, no one trying to make moves on him. He felt alone.

In the throne room

In the throne room, everyone was trying to find a way to get the princess back but nothing seemed to work.

Fedrick: (frustrated) There's nothing, NOTHING WE CAN DO!!! EVERY WAY LEADS TO THE BREAKING OF THAT DAMN TREATY!!!!

Cyrus: Calm down brother.

Fedrick: How do you expect me to calm down when our sister is there with that Maxwell!

Augustus: Fedrick we are trying okay and we all are worried for Cassandra, but that doesn't mean we'll lose

our patience. So calm down.

Fedrick doesn't stop and then three of the brothers start arguing with each other.

Seeing them fight Nikolai left the throne room. He was already very frustrated and seeing them fight for no reason was making him sick. He was missing the princess too much. In this 1 month, Nikolai decided that he'll not deny it anymore, he decided he'll accept the fact that he loves the princess, and he decided that when the princess will come back he'll happily embrace her and be with her.

At The Mordor Kingdom

In the past few days, the princess has been having this feeling. She hates Joseph and she knows it but whenever Joseph is around she can't just act like she hates him. She can't understand what she's feeling, she feels butterflies whenever she's around Joseph. At first, she thought it was just an attraction as Joseph is a hella attractive person. But that's not it, it's even stronger, even stronger than what she felt with Nikolai.........She can't decide whether it's hate or what. Because whatever it is, it's making her feel things she shouldn't.

Whereas Joseph has already fallen in love with the princess. Her innocence, her beauty, her attitude, her kindness, her politeness, everything made him fall for her. He knows it's not right he is supposed to hate her but he just can't help but love her. He knows she hates him and he is willing to go to extreme extents to make her fall in love with him.

"“He's willing to make love his top priority”"

9

The Confession 2.0

At the Mordor Kingdom

At the Dining Hall

It was morning, and the King and princess were having their breakfast. Cassandra was staring at Joseph for the last 5 minutes, she was thinking about her feelings but she didn't realize that she was directly staring at Joseph.

Joseph: Are you that in love with me princess that you can't even stop staring at me?

Cassandra: Pardon?

Joseph: (chuckles) Oh come on princess accept it. You are in love with me.

Cassandra: It-Its nothing like that.

Joseph: Your eyes are like mirrors to me. I can see my soul in them and I can find love for me in them.

Cassandra looks at him for a minute and then leaves.

Joseph: (shouts) I KNOW YOU LOVE ME!!

Cassandra blushes and goes to her room.

In her room

Cassandra: What is happening to me?? Why the hell did I blush!!?? GODDDD!!!!! What are you doing to me?? (sighs)

Few days later

Today Joseph has decided he'll propose Cassandra. He wanted to know about her feelings. He wanted to be with her.

It was night, the garden was decorated beautifully. There were flowers and candles everywhere. Joseph sends a maid to call Cassandra. When Cassandra came she was surprised and was about to say something but before she could Joseph spoke.

Joseph: Before you say something, I wanna tell you something. (takes a deep breath)

Joseph: Cassandra, You are the first ever person who came as sunlight in this dark room where I was locked for decades...I want to spend my whole life with you and I want you to be my first and last in everything. Though we had a drastic first meet... I want to spend my life peacefully with you. I know I am not perfect but I'll try my best to be worthy of you. I love you, Cassandra. Will you marry me? (takes out a ring from his pocket)

Cassandra: (shocked)Joseph WHAT ARE YOU SAYING!!!

Joseph: I love you, Cassandra. Please marry me...

Cassandra goes toward Joseph and SLAPPED HIM......

Cassandra: WHAT DO YOU THINK OF YOURSELF HUH!!! DO YOU THINK I'LL EVER MARRY A MAN WHO PLACED A SWORD AT MY FATHER'S NECK, WHO FORCED ME TO COME HERE WITH HIM, WHO SEPARATED ME FROM MY FAMILY!!!! DO REALLY THINK I'LL LOVE YOU!!!!

Cassandra leaves after saying this. Joseph looked at her disappearing. A tear escaped his eyes, he wiped it. It was the first time he cried. He felt broken.

The next day

Cassandra woke up to a maid shaking her. She saw all her room was cleared, and her things were not there.

Cassandra: What's happening??

Maid: Your majesty you can go to your castle now.

Cassandra: what do you mean???

Maid: The king ordered for you to be sent back to the Akkadian Kingdom.

Cassandra: He's sending me back......Where is he??

Maid: He left early in the morning and hasn't come back yet.

Cassandra: okay.

Cassandra got ready and left for her kingdom. She didn't know why she feels sad, she feels bad for being rude to Joseph but she did right. Right? How could she marry him he did so bad to her family...

At The Akkadian Kingdom

At the Castle

Cassandra enters the throne room. Everyone was shocked but soon the queen embraced her in a tight hug the other member of the royal family also joined her.

King Robert: Daughter are you okay?? How are you here?? Did you run?? What happened??

Cassandra: Father! Father! Calm down! I am fine and I didn't run he let me go.

Cyrus: He did??

Cassandra: Yes.

Fedrick: But why I mean he fought so much to take you with him.

Augustus: Yes Cassandra Fedricks Right. Did something happen??

Cassandra: No brother nothing happened. Maybe he just thought of doing some good in his life.

After this Cassandra went to her room to take some rest.

Suddenly she heard a knock on her window. She looked outside and saw..................

> ***"“A broken heart is the worst. It's like having broken ribs. Nobody can see it but the pain is unbearable every time you breathe.”"***

10

The Acceptance

Cassandra slowly walked towards the window, she removed the curtain and saw NIKOLAI. She quickly let him in. She was about to ask him what he was doing here but before she could Nikolai hugged her tightly.

Nikolai: I missed you so much, princess. I am so happy to see you back. I love you princess.

Cassandra was shocked. She was happy but something just didn't feel right. But she still hugged him back.

Cassandra: I missed you too Commander.

After talking a bit and confessing his feelings Nikolai left.

After Nikolai left. Cassandra felt bad as she didn't feel the same as she used to. She didn't feel love for him. She was feeling bad that when he finally confessed, she just couldn't feel it. It didn't seem right.

The next day

In the throne room

King Robert: Augustus have you informed everyone that we are attacking the Mordors?

Augustus: Yes father.

King Robert: Now that Maxwell will see the consequences of taking my daughter away.

Fedrick: But father is this necessary? I mean he did send her back and also he didn't harm her or something. Plus this will only lead to the breaking of the treaty.

King Robert: It is necessary Fedrick. Yes, he did send her back but he also did keep her there for 1 month. And about the treaty, it won't have any importance once I finish him.

Nikolai: Prince Fedrick, he took the princess away from her family. So he needs to face the consequences.

Fedrick: (sighs) You all can do whatever you want, but I am against this. (he leaves)

Augustus was about to stop him. But the king stopped him.

King Robert: It's okay Augustus, it's his opinion.

Augustus just nods.

At Night in the dining hall

Cassandra heard about what happened in the throne room. She hurriedly ran to the dining hall. The thought of Joseph getting hurt feared her. She went there and saw everyone having their dinner. Nikolai was also there.

Cassandra: Father!

King Robert: Yes Cassandra.

Cassandra: Ar-Are you going to attack the Mordors?

King Robert: Yes.

Cassandra: But why?

King Robert: What do mean by why, he took you away from us, so he needs to pay.

Cassandra: Yes but he also did send me back. He didn't even do any harm to me. Then what's the point of the war?

King Robert: Cassandra. We are going to attack the Mordors tomorrow and that's final. End of discussion.

The king was about to leave but Cassandra stopped him.

Cassandra: You can't attack them.

King Robert: And whys that?

Cassandra: Be-Because—

King Robert: BECAUSE WHAT??

Cassandra: BECAUSE I LOVE HIM!!!

She said it. She accepted she loved him. She accepted it.

King Robert/ Nikolai: WHAT!!!!

She looked at Nikolai with an apologetic face. Nikolai understood he was too late, her heart is already owned by someone else.

Cassandra: Father I love Joseph. So please understand.

Queen Alexandra: Cassandra what are you saying!!! How can you fall in love with someone like him?

Cassandra: I don't know mother!!! But I did and I am not gonna stop loving him.

King Robert: SHUT UP CASSANDRA!!!!

King Robert: He doesn't deserve to be loved. So stop loving him and go back to your room.

Cassandra: But Father—

King Robert: GO BACK TO YOUR ROOM!!!

Cassandra ran back to her room.

Cassandra cried her heart in her room. She felt so bad. She loved him and couldn't do anything to protect him. While crying she suddenly remembered Nikolai. She hurriedly went to Nikolai's room and knocked on the door.

In Nikolai's Room

He opened the door.

Nikolai: Princess.

Cassandra: I believe we need to talk.

Nikolai nodded. And let her in.

Cassandra: Look Nikolai I am sorry I just—

Nikolai: No Princess I understand. It took me such a long time. I understand.

Cassandra: No Nikolai I am really really sorry. I really loved you, it's just every time I tried to make you accept you didn't and I just......I don't know. I don't know when I stopped loving you. I don't know when I fell for him......H-He proposed me, and he asked me to marry him beside the fact that I am the princess of his rival kingdom, he took the risk.

Nikolai: Did you say yes?

Cassandra: No I couldn't because I still thought I loved you. But when yesterday you came to me at night and confessed, then I realized that I didn't love you anymore. (looked at Nikolai)I am sorry.

Nikolai: There's no need to be sorry princess. Love is not something we can control and I am happy that you accepted that you don't love me anymore, instead of forcing your feelings, because that would have destroyed 3 lives, yours, mine, and josephs. After all, love can't be forced.

Cassandra looked at him.

Nikolai: I understand princess. My breaking heart and I agree, that you and I could never be, so with me best........my very best, I set you free. I set you free princess and please don't feel bad that you and I couldn't be together because it's better to be with the person you love rather than being with someone with whom you have to force your feelings. And this is not the end this, is a thank you. Thank you for coming into my life and giving me joy, thank you for loving me. Thank you for the memories I will cherish forever.

Cassandra hugs him.

Cassandra: Thank you to you too. Thank you for understanding me and letting me go.

She smiles at him and leaves the room. After she leaves Nikolai cries because this was the first time he loved someone and he had to let her go.

11

The Revenge

The next day

The king told Cyrus to lock the princess in her room as he knew she would try to stop them. Cyrus locked her in the room. Cassandra begged him to open the door but he just said that it was for her best and left. Nikolai tried to convince the king not to attack as he couldn't see the princess in pain but it didn't help.

They attacked the Mordor kingdom. This time they had huge forces and were nicely prepared whereas the Mordors had no idea about the attack and were unprepared as their king was not okay. Joseph was too hurt and he was missing Cassandra too much that he forgot he has a kingdom to rule.

The Akkadians were already halfway towards the Mordor castle. They were defeating the Mordor army very easily. Whereas in the Akkadian kingdom, listening to the continuous begging and cries of her daughter the queen set Cassandra free. Cassandra thanked her mother and hurriedly went to the Mordor kingdom with Fedrick as he didn't go with the king. He didn't want to go but he couldn't let his sister go alone so he went with her.

King Robert and his army reached the castle and started fighting. Nikolai was fighting with the Mordor Commander, the king was fighting with Joseph, and Augustus and Cyrus were fighting with the rest of the army. King Robert was easily attacking Joseph as Joseph was not well, he felt mentally and physically weak as he didn't eat anything since the princess left. He couldn't fight because he was feeling so miserable. Nikolai defeated the Mordor commander and tied him to a pole. The king defeated Joseph and pushed him to his knees.

When Cassandra entered the castle she saw the Mordor army on the floor lying lifeless and Joseph on his knees in front of King Robert with the king's sword on his neck. Joseph was bleeding heavily. Cassandra ran inside.

Cassandra: JOSEPH!!!!!!

Joseph looked at him and smiled.

Joseph: You came my love.

Cassandra was about to go near him when Cyrus and Augustus stopped her.

Cassandra: Let me Go brothers.

Augustus: No Cassandra.

Cassandra: Nooooo!!!!!! Father tell them to let me go.

King Robert: I am sorry princess But I can't.

Cassandra: (fell on her knees) No Father, please.

King Robert: Cassandra the reason I locked you was to stop you from coming here and look at your lover getting killed by me. But you choose to come so I guess you'll have to see.

Cassandra: No father, please. (she cried)

Joseph: It's okay love. I can die happily knowing that you love me back. We have reached the end of our journey but I will never forget you. Farewell, dear one.

Cassandra: No please No!!!!!!

The king raised his sword and.................
Cassandra: NOOOOO!!!!!!!!!!!!!!!!!!!!

12

The Goodbye

Just when the king was about to kill Joseph, Nikolai looked at Cassandra and saw how miserable she was, he knew he had to do something so just when the sword was about to get struck Joseph he pushed Joseph aside and himself came in front of the sword and got struck.

Cassandra: NOOO!!!!!!!!!!!!!!!!!!!NIKOLAI!!!!!

Everybody looked at Nikolai and saw him fall to the ground with the sword struck right between his chest. Cassandra pushed her brothers and ran to Nikolai. She went to him and put his head on her lap.

Cassandra: No Nikolai No... Please don't leave me please(she cried)

Nikolai: I have to go princess(he coughs)I'll always love you and remember you. I am sorry it took me soo long to confess, I am sorry I made you wait soo much, I am sorry for everything. And when I am gone I want you to live a happy life with Joseph okay?

Cassandra nods while crying.

Nikolai:(looks at Joseph) Please keep her happy and give her the love I couldn't I am giving you the most precious thing of my life.

Joseph: I will.

Nikolai:(looks back at Cassandra) Princess you have to let me go okay? Letting go means realizing that some people are a part of your history but not a part of your destiny. Hmm.

Cassandra nods. Suddenly Nikolai starts to cough badly.

Nikolai: My time has come princess. Goodbye.

Cassandra: Goodbye. (smiles at him while crying)

As Nikolai closes his eyes. Cassandra stands up and looks at her father who was looking down. He was shocked to know about Nikolai and Cassandra but what shocked him, even more, was that Nikolai was dead, that too because of him. He always treated Nikolai as his own son. And now his son was dead because of him.

Cassandra: Are you happy now father? You ruined it. YOU RUINED EVERYTHING!!!!

The king looked at her for a second and then hugged her.

King Robert: I am sorry daughter. I should have listened to you I am sorry.

Cassandra: Father your sorry won't bring Nikolai back(she cried).

King Robert: I am sorry Cassandra please forgive me. I will spare joseph and go back to my kingdom and I promise I'll never attack the Mordors ever again.

Cassandra: Then go. Go back home.

The Akkadians went back. They take Nikolai's body with them. When they left Cassandra looked at Joseph and hugged him.

After a few minutes, they parted away. Cassandra looked at him.

Cassandra:(in her mind)The way he looked and stare at me right now, I see someone who will fight for me, protect me and love me. I see home.

Cassandra: I never intended to fall in love with u, but you took my heart and gave me yours. Something I didn't expect. Now I can't think of my life without you in it.

Joseph: I love you too princess.

2 weeks later Joseph and Cassandra got married.

2 years later

Cassandra: Wait! Wait! Nikolai! Don't Run You'll get hurt.

Just then a small cute 1-year-old baby boy turned around and giggled cutely at his mother. Cassandra smiled seeing her little boy giggling. She went to him and picked him up.

Cassandra: My baby Nikolai, don't you wanna sleep huh?

Nikolai giggled and snuggled into his mother's neck. Cassandra laughs. Just then Joseph enters the room.

Joseph: Oh well hello there my little prince and queen.

Cassandra: Joseph your son doesn't want to sleep. He wants to play all day long. God knows where he gets this much energy from.

Joseph:(chuckles) Well he got it from his father. (takes Nikolai) Okay my little prince, let's put you to sleep hmm.

Joseph takes Nikolai with him to the bed and lays down with him. Cassandra goes to the balcony and looks at the stars.

Cassandra:(while looking at the sky) Hey there Nikolai, I hope you are at peace. It's been 2 years since you died, but I still miss you the same. (a tear escapes her eye)

Cassandra looks at the sky one last time and goes inside and sleeps.

"“Some people are gone but never forgotten.”"

"“The hardest part of losing someone isn’t having to say goodbye but rather learning to live without them. Always trying to fill the void, the emptiness that’s left inside your heart when they go.”"

The End

9 798889 590705

Printed by Libri Plureos GmbH in Hamburg,
Germany